Who Will Help Santa?

Publisher: My Vision Works Publishing

Written by Gail A. Orange,M.S.L.S.

Illustrated by Kyle Smith

Printed in the United States of America

otocopying
Library of Congress Cataloging-in-Publication Date

Orange,M.S.L.S. Gail A.

Who Will Help Santa?

To my Grandchildren:
Cassia, Jaida, Mathieu and Maxwell

I would like to thank my daughter, Dara
for being my ears and strengthwhen I am weak.

Thank you Ronnie for making my dream of
becoming a children's book author come true.

Thank you Pat, Ida and the ladies of the
Fellowship Chapel book club.

Who Will Help Santa

By: Gail A. Orange, M.S.L.S.
Illustrator: Kyle Smith

Who will help Santa?

There are now seven billion people living
on planet earth.

Seven billion is far to many for Santa to visit in one night.

Who can help Santa deliver toys on
Christmas eve?

Santa could ask Paulie Polar bear. Paulie
is too tall to drive the sleigh.

Santa could ask Wallie Walrus. Wallie Walrus is too short to drive the sleigh.

Santa could ask Sylvester Seal.
Sylvester is afraid to fly in the sleigh.

Santa could ask Patti Penguin. Patti
likes to stay near the North Pole Lakes.

Santa is asking Mrs. Claus to help
deliver toys this Christmas Eve.

Mrs. Claus is happy to help deliver toys
on Christmas eve.

Mrs. Claus is getting her own sleigh and eight tiny reindeer.

What will Mrs. Claus name her reindeer?

What names would you give her reindeer?

Mrs. Claus will visit half of the boys and girls on planet earth.

While Santa will visit the other half.

On this Christmas Eve there will be two
sleighs delivering toys to all the good
boys and girls.
MERRY CHRISTMAS TO ALL...

...AND TO ALL A GOOD NIGHT!

Made in the USA
Charleston, SC
06 December 2016